Lewis Goldsmith

Memoirs of the Court of St. Cloud

Volume 7

Lewis Goldsmith

Memoirs of the Court of St. Cloud
Volume 7

1st Edition | ISBN: 978-3-75235-461-4

Place of Publication: Frankfurt am Main, Germany

Year of Publication: 2020

Outlook Verlag GmbH, Germany.

MEMOIRS OF THE COURT OF ST. CLOUD

By Lewis Goldsmith

Volume 7

LETTER XXIV.

PARIS, October, 1805.

MY LORD:—Though loudly complained of by the Cabinet of St. Cloud, the Cabinet of St. Petersburg has conducted itself in these critical times with prudence without weakness, and with firmness without obstinacy. In its connections with our Government it has never lost sight of its own dignity, and, therefore, never endured without resentment those impertinent innovations in the etiquette of our Court, and in the manner and language of our Emperor to the representatives of legitimate Sovereigns. Had similar becoming sentiments directed the councils of all other Princes and the behaviour of their Ambassadors here, spirited remonstrances might have moderated the pretensions or passions of upstart vanity, while a forbearance and silence, equally impolitic and shameful, have augmented insolence by flattering the pride of an insupportable and outrageous ambition.

The Emperor of Russia would not have been so well represented here, had he not been so wisely served and advised in his council chamber at St. Petersburg. Ignorance and folly commonly select fools for their agents, while genius and capacity employ men of their own mould, and of their own cast. It is a remarkable truth that, notwithstanding the frequent revolutions in Russia, since the death of Peter the First the ministerial helm has always been in able hands; the progressive and uninterrupted increase of the real and relative power of the Russian Empire evinces the reality of this assertion.

The Russian Chancellor, Count Alexander Woronzoff, may be justly called the chief of political veterans, whether his talents or long services are considered. Catherine II., though a voluptuous Princess, was a great Sovereign, and a competent judge of merit; and it was her unbiased choice that seated Count Woronzoff, while yet young, in her councils. Though the intrigues of favourites have sometimes removed him, he always retired with the esteem of his Sovereign, and was recalled without caballing or cringing to return. He is admired by all who have the honour of approaching him, as much for his obliging condescension as for his great information. No petty views, no petty caprices, no petty vengeances find room in his generous bosom. He is known to have conferred benefactions, not only on his enemies, but on those who, at the very time, were meditating his destruction. His opinion is that a patriotic Minister should regard no others as his enemies but those conspiring against their country, and acknowledge no friends or favourites incapable of well serving the State. Prince de Z——— waited on him one day, and, after hesitating some time, began to compliment him on his liberal sentiments, and concluded by asking the place of a governor for his cousin, with whom he had reason to suppose the Count much offended. "I am happy," said His Excellency, "to oblige you, and to do my duty at the same time. Here is a libel he wrote against me, and presented to the Empress, who graciously has communicated it to me, in answer to my recommendation of him yesterday to the place you ask for him to-day. Read what I have written on the libel, and you will be convinced that it will not be my fault if he is not to-day a governor." In two hours afterwards the nomination was announced to Prince de Z————, who was himself at the head of a cabal against the Minister. In any country such an act would have been laudable, but where despotism rules with unopposed sway, it is both honourable and praiseworthy.

Prince Adam Czartorinsky, the assistant of Count Woronzoff, and Minister of the foreign department, unites, with the vigour of youth, the experience of age. He has travelled in most countries of Europe, not solely to figure at Courts, to dance at balls, to look at pictures, or to collect curiosities, but to study the character of the people, the laws by which they are governed, and their moral or social influence with regard to their comforts or misery. He therefore brought back with him a stock of knowledge not to be acquired from books, but only found in the world by frequenting different and opposite societies with observation, penetration, and genius. With manners as polished as his mind is well informed, he not only, possesses the favour, but the friendship of his Prince, and, what is still more rare, is worthy of both. All Sovereigns have favourites, few ever had any friends; because it is more easy to flatter vanity, than to display a liberal disinterestedness; to bow meanly than to instruct or to guide with delicacy and dignity; to abuse the confidence of the Prince than to use it to his honour, and to the advantage of his Government.

That such a Monarch as an Alexander, and such Ministers as Count Woronzoff and Prince Czartorinsky, should appoint a Count Markof to a high and important post, was not unexpected by any one not ignorant of his merit.

Count Markof was, early in the reign of Catherine II., employed in the office of the foreign department at St. Petersburg, and was, whilst young, entrusted with several important negotiations at the Courts of Berlin and Vienna., when Prussia had proposed the first partition of Poland. He afterward went on his travels, from which he was recalled to fill the place of an Ambassador to the late King of Sweden, Gustavus III. He was succeeded, in 1784, at Stockholm, by Count Muschin Puschin, after being appointed a Secretary of State in his own country, a post he occupied with distinction, until the death of Catherine II., when Paul the First revenged upon him, as well as on most others of the faithful servants of this Princess, his discontent with his mother. He was then exiled to his estates, where he retired with the esteem of all those who had known him. In 1801, immediately after his accession to the throne, Alexander invited Count Markof to his Court and Council, and the trusty but difficult task of representing a legitimate Sovereign at the Court of our upstart usurper was conferred on him. I imagine that I see the great surprise of this nobleman, when, for the first time, he entered the audience-chamber of our little great man, and saw him fretting, staring, swearing, abusing to right and to left, for one smile conferring twenty frowns, and for one civil word making use of fifty hard expressions, marching in the diplomatic audience as at the head of his troops, and commanding foreign Ambassadors as his French soldiers. I have heard that the report of Count Markof to his Court, describing this new and rare show, is a chef-d'oeuvre of wit, equally amusing and instructive. He is said to have requested of his Cabinet new and particular orders how to act —whether as the representative of an independent Sovereign, or, as most of the other members of the foreign diplomatic corps in France, like a valet of the First Consul; and that, in the latter case, he implored as a favour, an immediate recall; preferring, had he no other choice left, sooner to work in the mines at Siberia than to wear, in France the disgraceful fetters of a Bonaparte. His subsequent dignified conduct proves the answer of his Court.

Talleyrand's craft and dissimulation could not delude the sagacity of Count Markof, who was, therefore, soon less liked by the Minister than by the First Consul. All kind of low, vulgar, and revolutionary chicanery was made use of to vex or to provoke the Russian Ambassador. Sometimes he was reproached with having emigrants in his service; another time protection was refused to one of his secretaries, under pretence that he was a Sardinian subject. Russian travellers were insulted, and detained on the most frivolous pretences. Two Russian noblemen were even arrested on our side of the Rhine, because Talleyrand had forgotten to sign his name to their passes, which were otherwise in order. The fact was that our Minister suspected them of carrying some papers which he wanted to see, and, therefore, wrote his name with an ink of such a composition that, after a certain number of days, everything written with it disappeared. Their effects and papers were strictly searched by an agent preceding them from this capital, but nothing was found, our Minister being misinformed by his spies.

When Count Markof left Sweden, he carried with him an actress of the French theatre at Stockholm, Madame Hus, an Alsatian by birth, but who had quitted her country twelve years before the Revolution, and could, therefore, never be included among emigrants. She had continued as a mistress with this nobleman, is the mother of several children by him, and an agreeable companion to him, who has never been married. As I have often said, Talleyrand is much obliged to any foreign diplomatic agent who allows him to be the indirect provider or procurer of his mistresses. After in vain tempting Count Markof with new objects, he introduced to the acquaintance of Madame Hus some of his female emissaries. Their manoeuvres, their insinuations, and even their presents were all thrown away. The lady remained the faithful friend, and therefore refused with indignation to degrade herself into a spy on her lover. Our Minister then first discovered that, not only was Madame Hus an emigrant, but had been a great benefactress and constant companion of emigrants at St. Petersburg, and, of course, deserved to be watched, if not punished. Count Markof is reported to have said to Talleyrand on this grave subject, in the presence of two other foreign Ambassadors:

"Apropos! what shall I do to prevent my poor Madame Hus from being shot as an emigrant, and my poor children from becoming prematurely orphans?"

"Monsieur," said our diplomatic oracle, "she should have petitioned the First Consul for a permission to return, to France before she entered it; but out of regard for you, if she is prudent, she will not, I daresay, be troubled by our Government."

"I should be sorry if she was not," replied the Count, with a significant look; and here this grand affair ended, to the great entertainment of those foreign agents who dared to smile or to laugh.

LETTER XXV.

MY LORD:—The Legion of Honour, though only proclaimed upon Bonaparte's assumption of the Imperial rank, dates from the first year of his consulate. To prepare the public mind for a progressive elevation of himself, and for consequential distinctions among all classes of his subjects, he distributed among the military, arms of honour, to which were attached precedence and privileges granted by him, and, therefore, liable to cease with his power or life. The number of these arms increased in proportion to the approach of the period fixed for the change of his title and the erection of his throne. When he judged them numerous enough to support his changes, he made all these wearers of arms of honour knights. Never before were so many chevaliers created en masse; they amounted to no less than twenty-two thousand four hundred, distributed in the different corps of different armies, but principally in the army of England. To these were afterwards joined five thousand nine hundred civil functionaries, men of letters, artists, etc. To remove, however, all ideas of equality, even among the members of the Legion of Honour, they were divided into four classes—grand officers, commanders, officers, and simple legionaries.

Every one who has observed Bonaparte's incessant endeavours to intrude himself among the Sovereigns of Europe, was convinced that he would cajole, or force, as many of them as he could into his revolutionary knighthood; but I heard men, who are not ignorant of the selfishness and corruption of our times, deny the possibility of any independent Prince suffering his name to be registered among criminals of every description, from the thief who picked the pockets of his fellow citizens in the street, down to the regicide who sat in judgment and condemned his King; from the plunderers who have laid waste provinces, republics, and kingdoms, down to the assassins who shot, drowned, or guillotined their countrymen en masse. For my part, I never had but one opinion, and, unfortunately, it has turned out a just one. I always was convinced that those Princes who received other presents from Bonaparte could have no plausible excuse to decline his ribands, crosses, and stars. But who could have presumed to think that, in return for these blood-stained baubles, they would have sacrificed those honourable and dignified ornaments which, for ages past, have been the exclusive distinction of what birth had exalted, virtue made eminent, talents conspicuous, honour illustrious, or valour meritorious? Who would have dared to say that the Prussian Eagle and the Spanish Golden Fleece should thus be prostituted, thus polluted? I do not mean by this remark to throw any blame on the conferring those and other orders on Napoleon Bonaparte, or even on his brothers; I know it is usual, between legitimate Sovereigns in alliance, sometimes to exchange their knighthoods; but to debase royal orders so much as to present them to a Cambaceres, a Talleyrand, a Fouche, a Bernadotte, a Fesch, and other vile and criminal wretches, I do not deny to have excited my astonishment as well as my indignation. What honest—I do not say what noble—subjects of Prussia, or of Spain, will hereafter think themselves rewarded for their loyalty, industry, patriotism, or zeal, when they remember that their Sovereigns have nothing to give but what the rebel has obtained, the robber worn, the murderer vilified, and the regicide debased?

The number of grand officers of the Legion of Honour does not yet amount to more than eighty, according to a list circulated at Milan last spring, of which I have seen a copy. Of these grand officers, three had been shoemakers, two tailors, four bakers, four barbers, six friars, eight abbes, six officers, three pedlers, three chandlers, seven drummers, sixteen soldiers, and eight regicides; four were lawful Kings, and the six others, Electors or Princes of the most ancient houses in Europe. I have looked over our, own official list, and, as far as I know, the calculation is exact, both with regard to the number and to the quality.

This new institution of knighthood produced a singular effect on my vain and giddy, countrymen, who, for twelve years before, had scarcely seen a star or a riband, except those of foreign Ambassadors, who were frequently insulted when wearing them. It became now the fashion to be a knight, and those who really were not so, put pinks, or rather blooms, or flowers of a darker red, in their buttonholes, so as to resemble, and to be taken at a distance for, the red ribands of the members of the Legion of Honour.

A man of the name of Villeaume, an engraver by profession, took advantage of this knightly fashion and mania, and sold for four louis d'or, not only the stars, but pretended letters of knighthood, said to be procured by his connection with persons of the household of the Emperor. In a month's time, according to a register kept by him, he had made twelve hundred and fifty knights. When his fraud was discovered, he was already out of the way, safe with his money; and, notwithstanding the researches of the police, has not since been taken.

A person calling himself Baron von Rinken, a subject and an agent of one of the many Princes of Hohenlohe, according to his own assertion, arrived here with real letters and patents of knighthood, which he offered for sale for three hundred livres. The stars of this Order were as large as the star of the grand officers of the Legion of Honour, and nearly resembled it; but the ribands were of a different colour. He had already disposed of a dozen of these stars, when he was taken up by the police and shut up in the Temple, where he still remains. Four other agents of inferior petty German Princes have also been arrested for offering the Orders of their Sovereigns for sale.

A Captain Rouvais, who received six wounds in his campaign under Pichegru in 1794, wore the star of the Legion of Honour without being nominated a knight. He has been tried by a military commission, deprived of his pension, and condemned to four years' imprisonment in irons. He proved that he had presented fourteen petitions to Bonaparte for obtaining this mark of distinction, but in vain; while hundreds of others, who had hardly seen an enemy, or, at the most, made but one campaign, or been once wounded, had succeeded in their demands. As soon as sentence had been pronounced against him, he took a small pistol from his pocket, and shot himself through the head, saying, "Some one else will soon do the same for Bonaparte."

A cobbler, of the name of Matthieu, either in a fit of madness or from hatred to the new order of things, decorated himself with the large riband of the Legion of Honour, and had an old star fastened on his coat. Thus accoutred, he went into the Palais Royal, in the middle of the day, got upon a chair, and began to speak to his audience of the absurdity of true republicans not being on a level, even under an Emperor, and putting on, like him, all his ridiculous ornaments. "We are here," said he, "either all grand officers, or there exist no grand officers at all; we have all fought and paid for liberty, and for the Revolution, as much as Bonaparte, and have, therefore, the same right and claim with him." Here a police agent and some gendarmes interrupted his eloquence by taking him into custody. When Fouche asked him what he meant by such rebellious behaviour, he replied that it was only a trial to see whether destiny had intended him to become an Emperor or to remain a cobbler. On the next day he was shot as a conspirator. I saw the unfortunate man in the Palais Royal; his eyes looked wild, and his words were often incoherent. He was certainly a subject more deserving a place in a madhouse than in a tomb.

Cambaceres has been severely reprimanded by the Emperor for showing too much partiality for the Royal Prussian Black Eagle, by wearing it in preference to the Imperial Legion of Honour. He was given to understand that, except for four days in the year, the Imperial etiquette did not permit any subjects to display their knighthood of the Prussian Order. In Madame Bonaparte's last drawing-room, before His Imperial Majesty set out for the Rhine, he was ornamented with the Spanish, Neapolitan, Prussian, and Portuguese orders, together with those of the French Legion of Honour and of the Italian Iron Crown. I have seen the Emperor Paul, who was also an amateur of ribands and stars, but never with so many at once. I have just heard that the Grand Master of Malta has presented Napoleon with the Grand Cross of the Maltese Order. This is certainly a negative compliment to him, who, in July, 1798, officially declared to his then sectaries, the Turks and Mussulmans, "that the Grand Master, Commanders, Knights, and Order of Malta existed no more."

I have heard it related for a certainty among our fashionable ladies, that the Empress of the French also intends to institute a new order of female knighthood, not of honour, but of confidence; of which all our Court ladies, all the wives of our generals, public functionaries, etc., are to be members. The Imperial Princesses of the Bonaparte family are to be hereditary grand officers, together with as many foreign Empresses, Queens, Princesses, Countesses, and Baronesses as can be bayoneted into this revolutionary sisterhood. Had the Continent remained tranquil, it would already have been officially announced by a Senatus Consultum. I should suppose that Madame Bonaparte, with her splendid Court and brilliant retinue of German Princes and Electors at Strasburg, need only say the word to find hundreds of princely recruits for her knighthood in petto. Her mantle, as a Grand Mistress of the Order of CONFIDENCE, has been already embroidered at Lyons, and those who have seen it assert that it is truly superb. The diamonds of the star on the mantle are valued at six hundred thousand livres.

LETTER XXVI.

PARIS, October, 1805.

MY LORD:—Since Bonaparte's departure for Germany, fifteen individuals have been brought here, chained, from La Vendee and the—Western Departments, and are imprisoned in the Temple. Their crime is not exactly known, but private letters from those countries relate that they were recruiting for another insurrection, and that some of them were entrusted as Ambassadors from their discontented countrymen to Louis XVIII. to ask for his return to France, and for the assistance of Russia, Sweden, and England to support his claims.

These are, however, reports to which I do not affix much credit. Had the prisoners in the Temple been guilty, or only accused of such crimes, they would long ago have been tortured, tried, and executed, or executed without a trial. I suppose them mere hostages arrested by our Government, as security for the tranquillity of the Chouan Departments during our armies' occupation elsewhere. We have, nevertheless, two movable columns of six thousand men each in the country, or in its vicinity, and it would be not only impolitic, but a cruelty, to engage or allure the unfortunate people of these wretched countries into any plots, which, situated as affairs now are, would be productive of great and certain evil to them, without even the probability of any benefit to the cause of royalty and of the Bourbons. I do not mean to say that there are not those who rebel against Bonaparte's tyranny, or that the Bourbons have no friends; on the contrary, the latter are not few, and the former very numerous. But a kind of apathy, the effect of unavailing resistance to usurpation and oppression, has seized on most minds, and annihilated what little remained of our never very great public spirit. We are tired of everything, even of our existence, and care no more whether we are governed by a Maximilian Robespierre or by a Napoleon Bonaparte, by a Barras or by Louis XVIII. Except, perhaps, among the military, or among some ambitious schemers, remnants of former factions, I do not believe a Moreau, a Macdonald, a Lucien Bonaparte, or any person exiled by the Emperor, and formerly popular, could collect fifty trusty conspirators in all France; at least, as long as our armies are victorious, and organized in their present formidable manner. Should anything happen to our present chief, an impulse may be given to the minds now sunk down, and raise our characters from their present torpid state. But until such an event, we shall remain as we are, indolent but submissive, sacrificing our children and treasures for a cause we detest, and for a man we abhor. I am sorry to say it, but it certainly does, no honour to my nation when one million desperados of civil and military banditti are suffered to govern, tyrannize, and pillage, at their ease and undisturbed, thirty millions of people, to whom their past crimes are known, and who have every reason to apprehend their future wickedness.

This astonishing resignation (if I can call it so, and if it does not deserve a worse name), is so much the more incomprehensible, as the poverty of the higher and middle classes is as great as the misery of the people, and, except those employed under Bonaparte, and some few upstart contractors or army commissaries, the greatest privations must be submitted to in order to pay the enormous taxes and make a decent appearance. I know families of five, six, and seven persons, who formerly were wealthy, and now have for a scanty subsistence an income of twelve or eighteen hundred livres—per year, with which they are obliged to live as they can, being deprived of all the resource that elsewhere labour offers to the industrious, and all the succours compassion bestows on the necessitous. You know that here all trade and all commerce are at a stand or destroyed, and the hearts of our modern rich are as unfeeling as their manners are vulgar and brutal.

A family of ci-devant nobles of my acquaintance, once possessing a revenue of one hundred and fifty thousand livres—subsist now on fifteen hundred livres—per year; and this sum must support six individuals—the father and mother, with four children! It does so, indeed, by an arrangement of only one poor meal in the day; a dinner four times, and a supper three times, in the week. They endure their distress with tolerable cheerfulness, though in the same street, where they occupy the garrets of a house, resides, in an elegant hotel, a man who was once their groom, but who is now a tribune, and has within these last twelve years, as a conventional deputy, amassed, in his mission to Brabant and Flanders, twelve millions of livres. He has kindly let my friend understand that his youngest daughter might be received as a chambermaid to his wife, being informed that she has a good education. All the four daughters are good musicians, good drawers, and very able with their needles. By their talents they supported their parents and themselves during their emigration in Germany; but here these are of but little use or advantage. Those upstarts who want instruction or works of this sort apply to the first, most renowned, and fashionable masters or mistresses; while others, and those the greatest number, cannot afford even to pay the inferior ones and the most cheap. This family is one of the many that regret having returned from their emigration. But, you may ask, why do they not go back again to Germany? First, it would expose them to suspicion, and, perhaps, to ruin, were they to demand passes; and if this danger or difficulty were removed, they have no money for such a long journey.

But this sort of penury and wretchedness is also common with the families of the former wealthy merchants and tradesmen. Paper money, a maximum, and requisitions, have reduced those that did not share in the crimes and pillage of the Revolution, as much as the proscribed nobility. And, contradictory as it may seem, the number of persons employed in commercial speculations has more than tripled since we experienced a general stagnation of trade, the consequence of war, of want of capital, protection, encouragement, and confidence; but one of the magazines of 1789 contained more goods and merchandize than twenty modern magazines put together. The expenses of these new merchants are, however, much greater than sixteen years ago, the profit less, and the credit still less than the profit. Hence numerous bankruptcies, frauds, swindling, forgeries, and other evils of immorality, extravagance, and misery. The fair and honest dealers suffer most from the intrusion of these infamous speculators, who expecting, like other vile men wallowing in wealth under their eyes, to make rapid fortunes, and to escape detection as well as punishment—commit crimes to soothe disappointment. Nothing is done but for ready money, and even bankers' bills, or bills accepted by bankers, are not taken in payment before the signatures are avowed by the parties concerned. You can easily conceive what confusion, what expenses, and what; loss of time these precautions must occasion; but the numerous forgeries and fabrications have made them absolutely necessary.

The farmers and landholders are better off, but they also complain of the heavy taxes, and low price paid for what they bring to the market, which frequently, for want of ready money, remains long unsold. They take nothing but cash in payment; for, notwithstanding the endeavours of our Government, the notes of the Bank of France have never been in circulation among them. They have also been subject to losses by the fluctuation of paper money, by extortions, requisitions, and by the maximum. In this class of my countrymen remains still some little national spirit and some independence of character; but these are far from being favourable to Bonaparte, or to the Imperial Government, which the yearly increase of taxes, and, above all, the conscription, have rendered extremely odious. You may judge of the great difference in the taxation of lands and landed property now and under our Kings, when I inform you that a friend of mine, who, in 1792, possessed, in one of the Western Departments, twenty-one farms, paid less in contribution for them all than he does now for the three farms he has recovered from the wreck of his fortune.

LETTER XXVII.

PARIS, October, 1805.

MY LORD:—In a military empire, ruled by a military despot, it is a necessary policy that the education of youth should also be military. In all our public schools or prytanees, a boy, from the moment of entering, is registered in a company, and regularly drilled, exercised, and reviewed, punished for neglect or fault according to martial law, and advanced if displaying genius or application. All our private schools that wish for the protection of Government are forced to submit to the same military rules, and, therefore, most of our conscripts, so far from being recruits, are fit for any service as soon as put into requisition. The fatal effects to the independence of Europe to be dreaded from this sole innovation, I apprehend, have been too little considered by other nations. A great Power, that can, without obstacle, and with but little expense, in four weeks increase its disposable military force from one hundred and twenty to one hundred and eighty thousand young men, accustomed to military duty from their youth, must finally become the master of all other or rival Powers, and dispose at leisure of empires, kingdoms, principalities, and republics. NOTHING CAN SAVE THEM BUT THE ADOPTION OF SIMILAR MEASURES FOR THEIR PRESERVATION AS HAVE BEEN ADOPTED FOR THEIR SUBJUGATION.

When l'Etat Militaire for the year 13 (a work containing the official statement of our military forces) was presented to Bonaparte by Berthier, the latter said: "Sire, I lay before Your Majesty the book of the destiny of the world, which your hands direct as the sovereign guide of the armies of your empire." This compliment is a truth, and therefore no flattery. It might as justly have been addressed to a Moreau, a Macdonald, a Le Courbe, or to any other general, as to Bonaparte, because a superior number of well disciplined troops, let them be well or even indifferently commanded, will defeat those inferior in number. Three to one would even overpower an army of giants. Add to it the unity of plans, of dispositions, and of execution, which Bonaparte enjoys exclusively over such a great number of troops, while ten, or perhaps fifty, will direct or contradict every movement of his opponents. I tremble when I meditate on Berthier's assertion; may I never live to see it realized, and to see all hitherto independent nations prostrated, acknowledge that Bonaparte and destiny are the same, and the same distributor of good and evil.

One of the bad consequences of this our military education of youth is a total absence of all religious and moral lessons. Arnaud had, last August, the courage to complain of this infamous neglect, in the National Institute. "The youth," said he, "receive no other instruction but lessons to march, to fire, to bow, to dance, to sit, to lie, and to impose with a good grace. I do not ask for Spartans or Romans, but we want Athenians, and our schools are only forming Sybarites." Within twenty-four hours afterwards, Arnaud was visited by a police agent, accompanied by two gendarmes, with an order signed by Fouche, which condemned him to reside at Orleans, and not to return to Paris without the permission of the Government,—a punishment regarded here as very moderate for such an indiscreet zeal.

A schoolmaster at Auteuil, near this capital, of the name of Gouron, had a private seminary, organized upon the footing of our former colleges. In some few months he was offered more pupils than he could well attend to, and his house shortly became very fashionable, even for our upstarts, who sent their children there in preference. He was ordered before Fouche last Christmas, and commanded to change the hours hitherto employed in teaching religion and morals, to a military exercise and instruction, as both more necessary and more salubrious for French youth. Having replied that such an alteration was contrary to his plan and agreement with the parents of his scholars, the Minister stopped him short by telling him that he must obey what had been prescribed by Government, or stand the consequences of his refractory spirit. Having consulted with his friends and patrons, he divided the hours, and gave half of the time usually allotted to religion or morality to the study of military exercise. His pupils, however, remained obstinate, broke the drum, and tore and burnt the colours he had bought. As this was not his fault, he did not expect any further disturbance, particularly after having reported to the police both his obedience and the unforeseen result. But last March his house was suddenly surrounded in the night by gendarmes, and some police agents entered it. All the boys were ordered to dress and to pack up their effects, and to follow the gendarmes to several other schools, where the Government had placed them, and of which their parents would be informed. Gouron, his wife, four ushers, and six servants, were all arrested and carried to the police office, where Fouche, after reproaching them for their fanatical behaviour, as he termed it, told them, as they were so fond of teaching religious and moral duties, a suitable situation had been provided for them in Cayenne, where the negroes stood sadly in need of their early arrival, for which reason they would all set out on that very morning for Rochefort. When Gouron asked what was to become of his property, furniture, etc., he was told that his house was intended by Government for a preparatory school, and would, with its contents, be purchased, and the amount paid him in lands in Cayenne. It is not necessary to say that this example of Imperial justice had the desired effect on all other refractory private schoolmasters.

The parents of Gouron's pupils were, with a severe reprimand, informed

14

where their sons had been placed, and where they would be educated in a manner agreeable to the Emperor, who recommended them not to remove them, without a previous notice to the police. A hatter, of the name of Maille, however, ordered his son home, because he had been sent to a dearer school than the former. In his turn he was carried before the police, and, after a short examination of a quarter of an hour, was permitted, with his wife and two children, to join their friend Gouron at Rochefort, and to settle with him at Cayenne, where lands would also be given him for his property, in France. These particulars were related to me by a neighbour whose son had, for two years previous to this, been under Gouron's care, but who was now among those placed out by our Government. The boy's present master, he said, was a man of a notoriously bad and immoral character; but he was intimidated, and weak enough to remain contented, preferring, no doubt, his personal safety to the future happiness of his child. In your country, you little comprehend what a valuable instrument terror has been in the hands of our rulers since the Revolution, and how often fear has been mistaken abroad for affection and content.

All these minutiae and petty vexations, but great oppressions, of petty tyrants, you may easily guess, take up a great deal of time, and that, therefore, a Minister of Police, though the most powerful, is also the most occupied of his colleagues. So he certainly is, but, last year, a new organization of this Ministry was regulated by Bonaparte; and Fouche was allowed, as assistants, four Counsellors of State, and an augmentation of sixty-four police commissaries. The French Empire was then divided into four arrondissements, with regard to the general police, not including Paris and its vicinity, inspected by a prefect of police under the Minister. Of the first of these arrondissements, the Counsellor of State, Real, is a kind of Deputy Minister; the Counsellor of State, Miot, is the same of the second; the Counsellor of State, Pelet de la Lozere, of the third; and the Counsellor of State, Dauchy, of the fourth. The secret police agents, formerly called spies, were also considerably increased.

LETTER XXVIII.

PARIS, October, 1805.

MY LORD:—Before Bonaparte set out for the Rhine, the Pope's Nuncio was for the first time publicly rebuked by him in Madame Bonaparte's drawing-room, and ordered loudly to write to Rome and tell His Holiness to think himself fortunate in continuing to govern the Ecclesiastical States, without interfering with the ecclesiastical arrangements that might be thought necessary or proper by the Government in France.

Bonaparte's policy is to promote among the first dignitaries of the Gallican Church the brothers or relatives of his civil or military supporters; Cambacere's brother is, therefore, an Archbishop and Cardinal, and one of Lebrun's, and two of Berthier's cousins are Bishops. As, however, the relatives of these Senators, Ministers, or generals, have, like themselves, figured in many of the scandalous and blasphemous scenes of the Revolution, the Pope has sometimes hesitated about sanctioning their promotions. This was the case last summer, when General Dessolles's brother was transferred from the Bishopric of Digne to that of Chambry, and Bonaparte nominated for his successor the brother of General Miollis, who was a curate of Brignoles, in the diocese of Aix. This curate had not only been one of the first to throw up his letters of priesthood at the Jacobin Club at Aix, but had also sacrilegiously denied the divinity of the Christian religion, and proposed, in imitation of Parisian atheists, the worship of a Goddess of Reason in a common prostitute with whom he lived. The notoriety of these abominations made even his parishioners at Brignoles unwilling to go to church, and to regard him as their pastor, though several of them had been imprisoned, fined, and even transported as fanatics, or as refractory.

During the negotiation with Cardinal Fesch last year, the Pope had been promised, among other things, that, for the future, his conscience should not be wounded by having presented to him for the prelacy any persons but those of the purest morals of the French Empire; and that all his objections should be attended to, in case of promotions; his scruples removed, or his refusal submitted to. When Cardinal Fesch demanded His Holiness's Bull for the curate Miollis, the Cardinal Secretary of State, Gonsalvi, showed no less than twenty acts of apostasy and blasphemy, which made him unworthy of such a dignity. To this was replied that, having obtained an indulgence in toto for what was past, he was a proper subject; above all, as he had the protection of the Emperor of the French. The Pope's Nuncio here then addressed himself to our Minister of the Ecclesiastical Department, Portalis, who advised him not to speak to Bonaparte of a matter upon which his mind had been made up; he, nevertheless, demanded an audience, and it was in consequence of this request that he, in his turn, became acquainted with the new Imperial etiquette and new Imperial jargon towards the representatives of Sovereigns. On the same evening the Nuncio expedited a courier to Rome, and I have heard to-day that the nomination of Miollis is confirmed by the Pope.

From this relatively trifling occurrence, His Holiness might judge of the intention of our Government to adhere to its other engagements; but at Rome, as well as in most other Continental capitals, the Sovereign is the dupe of the perversity of his Counsellors and Ministers, who are the tools, and not seldom the pensioners, of the Cabinet of St. Cloud.

But in the kingdom of Italy the parishes and dioceses are, if possible, still worse served than in this country. Some of the Bishops there, after having done duty in the National Guards, worn the Jacobin cap, and fought against their lawful Prince, now live in open adultery; and, from their intrigues, are the terror of all the married part of their flock. The Bishop of Pavia keeps the wife of a merchant, by whom he has two children; and, that the public may not be mistaken as to their real father, the merchant received a sum of money to establish himself at Brescia, and has not seen his wife for these two years past. General Gourion, who was last spring in Italy, has assured me that he read the advertisement of a curate after his concubine, who had eloped with another curate; and that the Police Minister at Milan openly licensed women to be the housekeepers of priests.

A grand vicar, Sarini, at Bologna, was, in 1796, a friar, but relinquished then the convent for the tent, and exchanged the breviary for the musket. He married a nun of one cloister, from whom he procured a divorce in a month, to unite himself with an Abbess of another, deserted by him in her turn for the wife of an innkeeper, who robbed and eloped from her husband. Last spring he returned to the bosom of the Church, and, by making our Empress a present of a valuable diamond cross, of which he had pillaged the statue of a Madonna, he obtained the dignity of a grand vicar, to the great edification, no doubt, of all those who had seen him before the altar or in the camp, at the brothel, or in the hospital.

Another grand vicar of the same Bishop, in the same city, of the name of Rami, has two of his illegitimate children as singing-boys in the same cathedral where he officiates as a priest. Their mother is dead, but her daughter, by another priest, is now their father's mistress. This incestuous commerce is so little concealed that the girl does the honours of the grand vicar's house, and, with naivete enough, tells the guests and visitors of her happiness in having succeeded her mother. I have this anecdote from an officer who heard her make use of that expression.

In France, our priests, I fear, are equally as debauched and unprincipled; but, in yielding to their vicious propensities, they take care to save the appearance of virtue, and, though their guilt is the same, the scandal is less. Bonaparte pretends to be severe against all those ecclesiastics who are accused of any irregularities after having made their peace with the Church. A curate of Picardy, suspected of gallantry, and another of Normandy, accused of inebriety, were last month, without further trial or ceremony than the report of the Minister Portalis, delivered over to Fouche, who transported them to Cayenne, after they had been stripped of their gowns. At the same time, Cardinal Cambaceres and Cardinal Fesch, equally notorious for their excesses, were taken no notice of, except that they were laughed at in our Court circles.

I am, almost every day, more and more convinced that our Government is totally indifferent about what becomes of our religious establishment when the present race of priests is extinguished; which, in the course of nature, must happen in less than thirty years. Our military system and our military education discourage all young men from entering into orders; while, at the same time, the army is both more honourable and more profitable than the Church. Already we want curates, though several have been imported from Germany and Spain, and, in some departments, four, and even six parishes have only one curate to serve them all. The Bishops exhort, and the parents advise their children to study theology; but then the law of conscription obliges the student of theology, as well as the student of philosophy, to march together; and, when once in the ranks, and accustomed to the licentiousness of a military life, they are either unwilling, unfit, or unworthy to return to anything else. The Pope, with all his entreaties, and with all his prayers, was unable to procure an exception from the conscription of young men preparing themselves for priesthood. Bonaparte always answered: "Holy Father, were I to consent to your demand, I should soon have an army of priests, instead of an army of soldiers." Our Emperor is not unacquainted with the real character and spirit of his Volunteers. When the Pope represented the danger of religion expiring in France, for want of priests to officiate at the altars, he was answered that Bonaparte, at the beginning of his consulate, found neither altars nor priests in France; that if his reign survived the latter, the former would always be standing, and survive his reign. He trusted that the chief of the Church would prevent them from being deserted. He assured him that when once he had restored the liberties of the seas, and an uninterrupted tranquillity on the Continent, he should attend more, and perhaps entirely, to the affairs of the Church. He consented, however, that the Pope might institute, in the Ecclesiastical States, a seminary for two hundred young

Frenchmen, whom he would exempt from military conscription. This is the stock from which our Church establishment is to be supplied!

LETTER XXIX.

PARIS, October, 1805.

MY LORD:—The short journey of Count von Haugwitz to Vienna, and the long stay of our Imperial Grand Marshal, Duroc, at Berlin, had already caused here many speculations, not quite corresponding with the views and, perhaps, interests of our Court, when our violation of the Prussian territory made our courtiers exclaim: "This act proves that the Emperor of the French is in a situation to bid defiance to all the world, and, therefore, no longer courts the neutrality of a Prince whose power is merely artificial; who has indemnities to restore, but no delicacy, no regard to claims." Such was the language of those very men who, a month before, declared "that His Prussian Majesty held the balance of peace or war in his hands; that he was in a position in which no Prussian Monarch ever was before; that while his neutrality preserved the tranquillity of the North of Germany, the South of Europe would soon be indebted to his powerful mediation for the return of peace."

The real cause of this alteration in our courtiers' political jargon has not yet been known; but I think it may easily be discovered without any official publication. Bonaparte had the adroitness to cajole the Cabinet of Berlin into his interest, in the first month of his consulate, notwithstanding his own critical situation, as well as the critical situation of France; and he has ever since taken care both to attach it to his triumphal car and to inculpate it indirectly in his outrages and violations. Convinced, as he thought, of the selfishness which guided all its resolutions, all his attacks and invasions against the law of nations, or independence of States, were either preceded or followed with some offers of aggrandizement, of indemnity, of subsidy, or of alliance. His political intriguers were generally more successful in Prussia than his military heroes in crossing the Rhine or the Elbe, in laying the Hanse Towns under contribution, or in occupying Hanover; or, rather, all these acts of violence and injustice were merely the effects of his ascendency in Prussia. When it is, besides, remembered what provinces Prussia accepted from his bounty, what exchange of presents, of ribands, of private letters passed between Napoleon the First and Frederick William III., between the Empress of the French and the Queen of Prussia, it is not surprising if the Cabinet of St. Cloud thought itself sure of the submission of the Cabinet of Berlin, and did not esteem it enough to fear it, or to think that it would have spirit enough to resent, or even honour to feel, the numerous Provocations offered.

Whatever Bonaparte and Talleyrand write or assert to the contrary, their gifts are only the wages of their contempt, and they despise more that State they thus reward than those nations at whose expense they are liberal, and with whose spoil they delude selfishness or meanness into their snares. The more legitimate Sovereigns descend from their true dignity, and a liberal policy, the nearer they approach the baseness of usurpation and the Machiavellism of rebellion. Like other upstarts, they never suffer an equal. If you do not keep yourself above them, they will crush you beneath them. If they have no reason to fear you, they will create some quarrel to destroy you.

It is said here that Duroc's journey to Berlin was merely to demand a passage for the French troops through the Prussian territory in Franconia, and to prevent the Russian troops from passing through the Prussian territory in Poland. This request is such as might have been expected from our Emperor and his Minister. Whether, however, the tone in which this curious negotiation with a neutral power was begun, or that, at last, the generosity of the Russian Monarch awakened a sense of duty in the Cabinet of Berlin, the arrival of our pacific envoy was immediately followed with warlike preparations. Fortunate, indeed, was it for Prussia to have resorted to her military strength instead of trusting any longer to our friendly assurances. The disasters that have since befallen the Austrian armies in Suabia, partly occasioned by our forced marches through neutral Prussia, would otherwise soon have been felt in Westphalia, in Brandenburgh, and in Pomerania. But should His Prussian Majesty not order his troops to act in conjunction with Russia, Austria, England, and Sweden, and that very soon, all efforts against Bonaparte will be vain, as those troops which have dispersed the Austrians and repulsed the Russians will be more than equal to master the Prussians, and one campaign may be sufficient to convince the Prussian Ministers of their folly and errors for years, and to punish them for their ignorance or selfishness.

Some preparations made in silence by the Marquis of Lucchesini, his affected absence from some of our late Court circles, and the number of spies who now are watching his hotel and his steps, seem to indicate that Prussia is tired of its impolitic neutrality, and inclined to join the confederacy against France. At the last assembly at our Prince Cambaceres's, a rumour circulated that preliminary articles for an offensive alliance with your country had already been signed by the Prussian Minister, Baron Von Hardenberg, on one side, and by your Minister to the Court of Berlin on the other; according to which you were to take sixty thousand Prussians and twelve thousand Hessians into your pay, for five years certain. A courier from Duroc was said to have brought this news, which at first made some impression, but it wore away by degrees; and our Government, to judge from the expressions of persons in its confidence, seems more to court than to fear a rupture with Prussia. Indeed, besides all other reasons to carry on a war in the North of Europe, Bonaparte's numerous and young generals are impatient to enrich themselves, as Italy,

Switzerland, Holland, and the South of Germany are almost exhausted.

LETTER XXX.

PARIS, October, 1805.

MY LORD:—The provocations of our Government must have been extraordinary indeed, when they were able to awaken the Cabinet of Berlin from its long and incomprehensible infatuation of trusting to the friendly intentions of honest Talleyrand, and to the disinterested policy of our generous Bonaparte. To judge its intents from its acts, the favour of the Cabinet of St. Cloud was not only its wish but its want. You must remember that, last year, besides his ordinary Ambassador, Da Lucchesini, His Prussian Majesty was so ill advised as to despatch General Knobelsdorff as his extra representative, to assist at Napoleon's coronation, a degradation of lawful sovereignty to which even the Court of Naples, though surrounded with our troops, refused to subscribe; and, so late as last June, the same Knobelsdorff did, in the name of his Prince, the honours at the reviews near Magdeburg, to all the generals of our army in Hanover who chose to attend there. On this occasion the King lodged in a farmhouse, the Queen in the house of the curate of Koestelith, while our sans-culotte officers, Bernadotte & Co., were quartered and treated in style at the castle of Putzbull, fitted up for their accommodation. This was certainly very hospitable, and very civil, but it was neither prudent nor politic. Upstarts, experiencing such a reception from Princes, are convinced that they are dreaded, because they know that they have not merit to be esteemed.

Do not confound this Knobelsdorff with the late Field-marshal of that name, who, in 1796, answered to a request which our then Ambassador at Berlin (Abbe Sieges) had made to be introduced to him, NON ET SANS PHRASE, the very words this regicide used when he sat in judgment on his King, and voted LA MORT ET SANS PHRASE. This Knobelsdorff is a very different character. He pretends to be equally conspicuous in the Cabinet as in the field, in the boudoir as in the study. A demi-philosopher, a demi-savant, a demi-gallant and a demi-politician, constitute, all taken together, nothing except an insignificant courtier. I do not know whether he was among those Prussian officers who, in 1798, CRIED when it was inserted in the public prints that the Grand Bonaparte had been killed in an insurrection at Cairo, but of this I am certain, that were Knobelsdorff to survive Napoleon the First, none of His Imperial Majesty's own dutiful subjects would mourn him more sincerely than this subject of the King of Prussia. He is said to possess a great share of the confidence of his King, who has already employed him in several diplomatic missions. The principal and most requisite qualities in a negotiator are political information, inviolable fidelity, penetrating but unbiased judgment, a dignified firmness, and condescending manners. I have not been often enough in the society of General Knobelsdorff to assert whether nature and education have destined him to illumine or to cloud the Prussian monarchy.

I have already mentioned in a former letter that it was Count von Haugwitz who, in 1792, as Prussian Ambassador at Vienna, arranged the treaty which then united the Austrian and Prussian Eagles against the Jacobin Cap of Liberty. It is now said in our diplomatic circle that his second mission to the same capital has for an object the renewal of these ties, which the Treaty of Basle dissolved; and that our Government, to impede his success, or to occasion his recall, before he could have time to conclude, had proposed to Prussia an annual subsidy of thirty millions of liveres—which it intended to exact from Portugal for its neutrality. The present respectable appearance of Prussia, shows, however, that whether the mission of Haugwitz had the desired issue or not, His Prussian Majesty confides in his army in preference to our parchments.

Some of our politicians pretend that the present Minister of the foreign department in Prussia, Baron von Hardenberg, is not such a friend of the system of neutrality as his predecessor. All the transactions of his administration seem, nevertheless, to proclaim that, if he wished his country to take an active part in the present conflict, it would not have been against France, had she not begun the attack with the invasion of Anspach and Bayreuth. Let it be recollected that, since his Ministry, Prussia has acknowledged Bonaparte an Emperor of the French, has exchanged orders with him, and has sent an extraordinary Ambassador to be present at his coronation,—not common compliments, even between Princes connected by the nearest ties of friendship and consanguinity. Under his administration, the Rhine has been passed to seize the Duc d'Enghien, and the Elbe to capture Sir George Rumbold; the Hanse Towns have been pillaged, and even Emden blockaded; and the representations against, all these outrages have neither been followed by public reparation nor a becoming resentment; and was it not also Baron von Hardenberg, who, on the 5th of April, 1795, concluded at Basle that treaty to which we owe all our conquests and Germany and Italy all their disasters? It is not probable that the parent of pacification will destroy its own progeny, if self-preservation does not require it.

Baron von Hardenberg is both a learned nobleman and an enlightened statesman, and does equal honour both to his own rank and to the choice of his Prince. The late Frederick William II. nominated him a Minister of State and a Counsellor of his Cabinet. On the 26th of January, 1792, as a directorial

Minister, he took possession, in the name of the King of Prussia, of the Margravates of Anspach and Bayreuth, and the inhabitants swore before him, as their governor, their oaths of allegiance to their new Sovereign.—He continued to reside as a kind of viceroy, in these States, until March, 1795, when he replaced Baron von Goltz as negotiator with our republican plenipotentiary in Switzerland; but after settling all differences between Prussia and France, he returned to his former post at Anspach, where no complaints have been heard against his Government.

The ambition of Baron von Hardenberg has always been to obtain the place he now occupies, and the study of his life has been to gain such information as would enable him to fill it with distinction. I have heard it said that in most countries he had for years kept and paid private agents, who regularly corresponded with him and sent him reports of what they heard or saw of political intrigue or machinations. One of these his agents I happened to meet with, in 1796, at Basle, and were I to conclude from what I observed in him, the Minister has not been very judicious in his selection of private correspondents. Figure to yourself a bald-headed personage, about forty years of age, near seven feet high, deaf as a post, stammering and making convulsive efforts to express a sentence of five words, which, after all, his gibberish made unintelligible. His dress was as eccentric as his person was singular, and his manners corresponded with both. He called himself Baron von Bulow, and I saw him afterwards, in the autumn of 1797, at Paris, with the same accoutrements and the same jargon, assuming an air of diplomatic mystery, even while displaying before me, in a coffee-house, his letters and instructions from his principal. As might be expected, he had the adroitness to get himself shut up in the Temple, where, I have been told, the generosity of your Sir Sidney Smith prevented him from starving.

No member of the foreign diplomatic corps here possesses either more knowledge, or a longer experience, than the Prussian Ambassador, Marquis of Lucchesini. He went with several other philosophers of Italy to admire the late hero of modern philosophy at Berlin, Frederick the Great, who received him well, caressed him often, but never trusted or employed him. I suppose it was not at the mention of the Marquis's name for the place of a governor of some province that this Monarch said, "My subjects of that province have always been dutiful; a philosopher shall never rule in my name but over people with whom I am discontented, or whom I intend to chastise." This Prince was not unacquainted with the morality of his sectaries.

During the latter part of the life of this King, the Marquis of Lucchesini was frequently of his literary and convivial parties; but he was neither his friend nor his favourite, but his listener. It was first under Frederick William II. that he began his diplomatic career, with an appointment as Minister from Prussia to the late King of Poland. His first act in this post was a treaty signed on the 29th of March, 1790, with the King and Republic of Poland, which changed an elective monarchy into an hereditary one; but, notwithstanding the Cabinet of Berlin had guaranteed this alteration, and the constitution decreed in consequence, in 1791, three years afterwards Russian and Prussian bayonets annihilated both, and selfishness banished faith.

In July, 1790, he assisted as a Prussian plenipotentiary at the conferences at Reichenback, together with the English and Dutch Ambassadors, having for object a pacification between Austria and Turkey. In December of the same year he went with the same Ministers to the Congress at Sistova, where, in May, 1791, he signed the Treaty of Peace between the Grand Seignior and the Emperor of Germany. In June, 1792, he was a second time sent as a Minister to Warsaw, where he remained until January, 1793, when he was promoted to the post of Ambassador at the Court of Vienna. He continued, however, to reside with His Prussian Majesty during the greatest part of the campaign on the Rhine, and signed, on the 24th of June, 1793, in the camp before Mentz, an offensive and defensive alliance with your Court; an alliance which Prussian policy respected not above eighteen months. In October, 1796, he requested his recall, but this his Sovereign refused, with the most gracious expressions; and he could not obtain it until March, 1797. Some disapprobation of the new political plan introduced by Count von Haugwitz in the Cabinet at Berlin is supposed to have occasioned his determination to retire from public employment. As he, however, continued to reside in the capital of Prussia, and, as many believed, secretly intrigued to appear again upon the scene, the nomination, in 1800, to his present important post was as much the consequence of his own desire as of the favour of his King.

The Marquis of Lucchesini lives here in great style at the beautiful Hotel de l'Infantado, where his lady's routs, assemblies, and circles are the resort of our most fashionable gentry. Madame da Lucchesini is more agreeable than handsome, more fit to shine at Berlin than at Paris; for though her manners are elegant, they want that ease, that finish which a German or Italian education cannot teach, nor a German or Italian society confer. To judge from the number of her admirers, she seems to know that she is married to a philosopher. Her husband was born at Lucca, in Italy, and is, therefore, at present a subject of Bonaparte's brother-in-law, Prince Bacciochi, to whom, when His Serene Highness was a marker at a billiard-table, I have had the honour of giving many a shilling, as well as many a box on the ear.

LETTER XXXI.

PARIS, October, 1805.

MY LORD:—The unexampled cruelty of our Government to your countryman, Captain Wright, I have heard reprobated, even by some of our generals and public functionaries, as unjust as well as disgraceful. At a future General Congress, should ever Bonaparte suffer one to be convoked, except under his auspices and dictature, the distinction and treatment of prisoners of war require to be again regulated, that the valiant warrior may not for the future be confounded with, and treated as, a treacherous spy; nor innocent travellers, provided with regular passes, visiting a country either for business or for pleasure, be imprisoned, like men taken while combating with arms in their hands.

You remember, no doubt, from history, that many of our ships—that, during the reigns of George I. and II., carried to Ireland and Scotland, and landed there, the adherents and partisans of the House of Stuart were captured on their return or on their passage; and that your Government never seized the commanders of these vessels, to confine them as State criminals, much less to torture or murder them in the Tower. If I am not mistaken, the whole squadron which, in 1745, carried the Pretender and his suite to Scotland, was taken by your cruisers; and the officers and men experienced no worse or different treatment than their fellow prisoners of war; though the distance is immense between the crime of plotting against the lawful Government of the Princes of the House of Brunswick, and the attempt to disturb the usurpation of an upstart of the House of Bonaparte. But, even during the last war, how many of our ships of the line, frigates, and cutters, did you not take, which had landed rebels in Ireland, emissaries in Scotland, and malefactors in Wales; and yet your generosity prevented you from retaliating, even at the time when your Sir Sidney Smith, and this same unfortunate Captain Wright, were confined in our State prison of the Temple! It is with Governments as with individuals, they ought to be just before they are generous. Had you in 1797, or in 1798, not endured our outrages so patiently, you would not now have to lament, nor we to blush for, the untimely end of Captain Wright.

From the last time that this officer had appeared before the criminal tribunal which condemned Georges and Moreau, his fate was determined on by our Government. His firmness offended, and his patriotism displeased; and as he seemed to possess the confidence of his own Government, it was judged that he was in its secrets; it was, therefore, resolved that, if he refused to become a traitor, he should perish a victim. Desmarets, Fouche's private secretary, who is also the secretary of the secret and haute police, therefore ordered him to another private interrogatory. Here he was offered a considerable sum of money, and the rank of an admiral in our service, if he would divulge what he knew of the plans of his Government, of its connections with the discontented in this country, and of its means of keeping up a correspondence with them. He replied, as might have been expected, with indignation, to such offers and to such proposals, but as they were frequently repeated with new allurements, he concluded with remaining silent and giving no answers at all. He was then told that the torture would soon restore him his voice, and some select gendarmes seized him and laid him on the rack; there he uttered no complaint, not even a sigh, though instruments the most diabolical were employed, and pains the most acute must have been endured. When threatened that he should expire in torments, he said:

"I do not fear to die, because my country will avenge my murder, while my God receives my soul." During the two hours of the first day that he was stretched on the rack, his left arm and right leg were broken, and his nails torn from the toes of both feet; he then passed into the hands of a surgeon, and was under his care for five weeks, but, before he was perfectly cured, he was carried to another private interrogatory, at which, besides Desmarets, Fouche and Real were present.

The Minister of Police now informed him that, from the mutilated state of his body, and from the sufferings he had gone through, he must be convinced that it was not the intention of the French Government ever to restore him to his native country, where he might relate occurrences which the policy of France required to be buried in oblivion; he, therefore, had no choice between serving the Emperor of the French, or perishing within the walls of the prison where he was confined. He replied that he was resigned to his destiny, and would die as he had lived, faithful to his King and to his country.

The man in full possession of his mental qualities and corporeal strength is, in most cases, very different from that unfortunate being whose mind is, enervated by sufferings and whose body is weakened by wants. For five months Captain Wright had seen only gaolers, spies, tyrants, executioners, fetters, racks, and other tortures; and for five weeks his food had been bread and his drink water. The man who, thus situated and thus perplexed, preserves his native dignity and innate sentiments, is more worthy of monuments, statues, or altars than either the legislator, the victor, or the saint.

This interrogatory was the last undergone by Captain Wright. He was then again stretched on the rack, and what is called by our regenerators the INFERNAL torments, were inflicted on him. After being pinched with red-hot irons all over his body, brandy, mixed with gunpowder, was infused in the numerous wounds and set fire to several times until nearly burned to the bones. In the convulsions, the consequence of these terrible sufferings, he is said to have bitten off a part of his tongue, though, as before, no groans were heard. As life still remained, he was again put under the care of his former surgeon; but, as he was exceedingly exhausted, a spy, in the dress of a Protestant clergyman, presented himself as if to read prayers with him. Of this offer he accepted; but when this man began to ask some insidious questions, he cast on him a look of contempt and never spoke to him more. At last, seeing no means to obtain any information from him, a mameluke last week strangled him in his bed. Thus expired a hero whose fate has excited more compassion, and whose character has received more admiration here, than any of our great men who have fallen fighting for our Emperor. Captain Wright has diffused new rays of renown and glory on the British name, from his tomb as well as from his dungeon.

You have certainly a right to call me to an account for all the particulars I have related of this scandalous and abominable transaction, and, though I cannot absolutely guarantee the truth of the narration, I am perfectly satisfied of it myself, and I hope to explain myself to your satisfaction. Your unfortunate countryman was attended by and under the care of a surgeon of the name of Vaugeard, who gained his confidence, and was worthy of it, though employed in that infamous gaol. Either from disgust of life, or from attachment to Captain Wright, he survived him only twelve hours, during which he wrote the shocking details I have given you, and sent them to three of the members of the foreign diplomatic corps, with a prayer to have them forwarded to Sir Sidney Smith or to Mr. Windham, that those his friends might be informed that, to his last moment, Captain Wright was worthy of their protection and kindness. From one of those Ministers I have obtained the original in Vaugeard's own handwriting.

I know that Bonaparte and Talleyrand promised the release of Captain Wright to the Spanish Ambassador; but, at that time, he had already suffered once on the rack, and this liberality on their part was merely a trick to impose upon the credulity of the Spaniard or to get rid of his importunities. Had it been otherwise, Captain Wright, like Sir George Rumbold, would himself have been the first to announce in your country the recovery of his liberty.

LETTER XXXII.

PARIS, October, 1805.

My LORD:—Should Bonaparte again return here victorious, and a pacificator, great changes in our internal Government and constitution are expected, and will certainly occur. Since the legislative corps has completed the Napoleon code of civil and criminal justice, it is considered by the Emperor not only as useless, but troublesome and superfluous. For the same reasons the tribunate will also be laid aside, and His Majesty will rule the French Empire, with the assistance of his Senate, and with the advice of his Council of State, exclusively. You know that the Senators, as well as the Councillors of State, are nominated by the Emperor; that he changes the latter according to his whim, and that, though the former, according to the present constitution, are to hold their offices for life, the alterations which remove entirely the legislature and the tribunate may also make Senators movable. But as all members of the Senate are favourites or relatives, he will probably not think it necessary to resort to such a measure of policy.

In a former letter I have already mentioned the heterogeneous composition of the Senate. The tribunate and legislative corps are worthy to figure by its side; their members are also ci-devant mechanics of all descriptions, debased attorneys or apostate priests, national spoilers or rebellious regicides, degraded nobles or dishonoured officers. The nearly unanimous vote of these corps for a consulate for life, and for an hereditary Emperor, cannot, therefore, either be expressive of the national will, or constitute the legality of Bonaparte's sovereignty.

In the legislature no vote opposed, and no voice declaimed against, Bonaparte's Imperial dignity; but in the tribunate, Carnot—the infamously notorious Carnot—'pro forma', and with the permission of the Emperor 'in petto', spoke against the return of a monarchical form of Government. This farce of deception and roguery did not impose even on our good Parisians, otherwise, and so frequently, the dupes of all our political and revolutionary mountebanks. Had Carnot expressed a sentiment or used a word not previously approved by Bonaparte, instead of reposing himself in the tribunate, he would have been wandering in Cayenne.

Son of an obscure attorney at Nolay, in Burgundy, he was brought up, like Bonaparte, in one of those military schools established by the munificence of the French Monarchs; and had obtained, from the late King, the commission of a captain of engineers when the Revolution broke out. He was particularly indebted to the Prince of Conde for his support during the earlier part of his life, and yet he joined the enemies of his house, and voted for the death of Louis XVI. A member, with Robespierre and Barrere, of the Committee of Public Safety, he partook of their power, as well as of their crimes, though he has been audacious enough to deny that he had anything to do with other transactions than those of the armies. Were no other proofs to the contrary collected, a letter of his own hand to the ferocious Lebon, at Arras, is a written evidence which he is unable to refute. It is dated November 16th, 1793. "You must take," says he, "in your energy, all measures of terror commanded or required by present circumstances. Continue your revolutionary attitude; never mind the amnesty pronounced with the acceptance of the absurd constitution of 1791; it is a crime which cannot extenuate other crimes. Anti-republicans can only expiate their folly under the age of the guillotine. The public Treasury will always pay the journeys and expenses of informers, because they have deserved well of their country. Let all suspected traitors expire by the sword or by fire; continue to march upon that revolutionary line so well delineated by you. The committee applauds all your undertakings, all your measures of vigour; they are not only all permitted, but commanded by your mission." Most of the decrees concerning the establishment of revolutionary tribunals, and particularly that for the organization of the atrocious military commission at Orange, were signed by him.

Carnot, as an officer of engineers, certainly is not without talents; but his presumption in declaring himself the sole author of those plans of campaign which, during the years 1794, 1795, and 1796, were so triumphantly executed by Pichegru, Moreau, and Bonaparte, is impertinent, as well as unfounded. At the risk of his own life, Pichegru entirely altered the plan sent him by the Committee of Public Safety; and it was Moreau's masterly retreat, which no plan of campaign could prescribe, that made this general so famous. The surprising successes of Bonaparte in Italy were both unexpected and unforeseen by the Directory; and, according to Berthier's assertion, obliged the, commander-in-chief, during the first four months, to change five times his plans of proceedings and undertakings.

During his temporary sovereignty as a director, Carnot honestly has made a fortune of twelve millions of livres; which has enabled him not only to live in style with his wife, but also to keep in style two sisters, of the name of Aublin, as his mistresses. He was the friend of the father of these girls, and promised him, when condemned to the guillotine in 1793, to be their second father; but he debauched and ruined them both before either was fourteen years of age; and young Aublin, who, in 1796, reproached him with the infamy of his conduct, was delivered up by him to a military commission, which condemned him to be shot as an emigrant. He has two children by each of these unfortunate girls.

Bonaparte employs Carnot, but despises and mistrusts him; being well aware that, should another National Convention be convoked, and the Emperor of the French be arraigned, as the King of France was, he would, with as great pleasure, vote for the execution of Napoleon the First as he did for that of Louis XVI. He has waded too far in blood and crime to retrograde.

To this sample of a modern tribune I will add a specimen of a modern legislator. Baptiste Cavaignae was, before the Revolution, an excise officer, turned out of his place for infidelity; but the department of Lot electing him, in 1792, a representative of the people to the National Convention, he there voted for the death of Louis XVI. and remained a faithful associate of Marat and Robespierre. After the evacuation of Verdun by the Prussians, in October, 1792, he made a report to the Convention, according to which eighty-four citizens of that town were arrested and executed. Among these were twenty-two young girls, under twenty years of age, whose crime was the having presented nosegays to the late King of Prussia on his entry after the surrender of Verdun. He was afterwards a national commissary with the armies on the coast near Brest, on the Rhine, and in Western Pyrenees, and everywhere he signalized himself by unheard of ferocities and sanguinary deeds. The following anecdote, printed and published by our revolutionary annalist, Prudhomme, will give you some idea of the morality of this our regenerator and Imperial Solon: "Cavaignac and another deputy, Pinet," writes Prudhomme, "had ordered a box to be kept for them at the play-house at Bayonne on the evening they expected to arrive in that town. Entering very late, they found two soldiers, who had seen the box empty, placed in its front. These they ordered immediately to be arrested, and condemned them, for having outraged the national representation, to be guillotined on the next day, when they both were accordingly executed!" Labarrere, a provost of the Marechaussee at Dax, was in prison as a suspected person. His daughter, a very handsome girl of seventeen, lived with an aunt at Severe. The two pro-consuls passing through that place, she threw herself at their feet, imploring mercy for her parent. This they not only promised, but offered her a place in their carriage to Dax, that she might see him restored to liberty. On the road the monsters insisted on a ransom for the blood of her father. Waiting, afflicted and ashamed, at a friend's house at Dag, the accomplishment of a promise so dearly purchased, she heard the beating of the alarm drum, and looked, from curiosity, through the window, when she saw her unfortunate parent ascending the scaffold! After having remained lifeless for half an hour, she recovered her senses an instant, when she exclaimed:

31

"Oh, the barbarians! they violated me while flattering me with the hope of saving my father!" and then expired. In October, 1795, Cavaignac assisted Barras and Bonaparte in the destruction of some thousands of men, women, and children in the streets of this capital, and was, therefore, in 1796, made by the Directory an inspector-general of the customs; and, in 1803, nominated by Bonaparte a legislator. His colleague, Citizen Pinet, is now one of our Emperor's Counsellors of State, and both are commanders of His Majesty's Legion of Honour; rich, respected, and frequented by our most fashionable ladies and gentlemen.

LETTER XXXIII.

PARIS, October, 1805.

MY LORD:—I suppose your Government too vigilant and too patriotic not to be informed of the great and uninterrupted activity which reigns in our arsenals, dockyards, and seaports. I have seen a plan, according to which Bonaparte is enabled, and intends, to build twenty ships of the line and ten frigates, besides cutters, in the year, for ten years to come. I read the calculation of the expenses, the names of the forests where the timber is to be cut, of the foreign countries where a part of the necessary materials are already engaged, and of our own departments which are to furnish the remainder. The whole has been drawn up in a precise and clear manner by Bonaparte's Maritime Prefect at Antwerp, M. Malouet, well known in your country, where he long remained as an emigrant, and, I believe, was even employed by your Ministers.

You may, perhaps, smile at this vast naval scheme of Bonaparte; but if you consider that he is the master of all the forests, mines, and productions of France, Italy, and of a great part of Germany, with all the navigable rivers and seaports of these countries and Holland, and remember also the character of the man, you will, perhaps, think it less impracticable. The greatest obstacle he has to encounter, and to remove, is want of experienced naval officers, though even in this he has advanced greatly since the present war, during which he has added to his naval forces twenty—nine ships of the line, thirty —four frigates, twenty-one cutters, three thousand prams, gunboats, pinnaces, etc., with four thousand naval officers and thirty-seven thousand sailors, according to the same account, signed by Malouet. It is true that most of our new naval heroes have never ventured far from our coast, and all their naval laurels have been gathered under our land batteries; but the impulse is given to the national spirit, and our conscripts in the maritime departments prefer, to a man, the navy to the army, which was not formerly the case.

It cannot have escaped your observation that the incorporation of Genoa procured us, in the South of our Empire, a naval station and arsenal, as a counterpoise to Antwerp, our new naval station in the North, where twelve ships of the line have been built, or are building, since 1803, and where timber and other materials are collected for eight more. At Genoa, two ships of the line and four frigates have lately been launched, and four ships and two frigates are on the stocks; and the Genoese Republic has added sixteen thousand seafaring men to our navy. Should Bonaparte terminate successfully the present war, Naples and Venice will increase the number of our seaports and resources on the borders of the Mediterranean and Adriatic Seas. All his courtiers say that he will conquer Italy in Germany, and determine at Vienna —the fate of London.

Of all our admirals, however, we have not one to compare with your Nelson, your Hood, your St. Vincent, and your Cornwallis. By the appointment of Murat as grand admiral, Bonaparte seems to indicate that he is inclined to imitate the example of Louis. XVI., in the beginning of his reign, and entrust the chief command of his fleets and squadrons to military men of approved capacity and courage, officers of his land troops. Last June, when he expected a probable junction of the fleet under Villeneuve with the squadron under Admiral Winter, and the union of both with Ganteaume at Brest, Murat was to have had the chief command of the united French, Spanish, and Batavian fleets, and to support the landing of our troops in your country; but the arrival of Lord Nelson in the West Indies, and the victory of Admiral Calder, deranged all our plans and postponed all our designs, which the Continental war has interrupted; to be commenced, God knows when.

The best amongst our bad admirals is certainly Truguet; but he was disgraced last year, and exiled twenty leagues from the coast, for having declared too publicly "that our flotillas would never be serviceable before our fleets were superior to yours, when they would become useless." An intriguer by long habit and by character, having neither property nor principles, he joined the Revolution, and was the second in command under Latouche, in the first republican fleet that left our harbours. He directed the expedition against Sardinia, in January, 1793, during which he acquired neither honour nor glory, being repulsed with great loss by the inhabitants. After being imprisoned under Robespierre, the Directory made him a Minister of the marine, an Ambassador to Spain, and a Vice-Admiral of France. In this capacity he commanded at Brest, during the first eighteen months of the present war. He has an irreconcilable foe in Talleyrand, with whom he quarrelled, when on his embassy in Spain, about some extortions at Madrid, which he declined to share with his principal at Paris. Such was our Minister's inveteracy against him in 1798, that a directorial decree placed him on the list of emigrants, because he remained in Spain after having been recalled to France. In 1799, during Talleyrand's disgrace, Truguet returned here, and, after in vain challenging his enemy to fight, caned him in the Luxembourg gardens, a chastisement which our premier bore with true Christian patience. Truguet is not even a member of the Legion of Honour.

Villeneuve is supposed not much inferior in talents, experience, and modesty to Truguet. He was, before the Revolution, a lieutenant of the royal navy; but his principles did not prevent him from deserting to the colours of the enemies of royalty, who promoted him first to a captain and afterwards to an admiral.

His first command as such was over a division of the Toulon fleet, which, in the winter of 1797, entered Brest. In the battle at Aboukir he was the second in command; and, after the death of Admiral Brueys, he rallied the ships which had escaped, and sailed for Malta, where, two years afterwards, he signed, with General Vaubois, the capitulation of that island. When hostilities again broke out, he commanded in the West Indies, and, leaving his station, escaped your cruisers, and was appointed first to the chief command of the Rochefort, and afterwards the Toulon fleet, on the death of Admiral Latouche. Notwithstanding the gasconade of his report of his negative victory over Admiral Calder, Villeneuve is not a Gascon by birth, but only, by sentiment.

Ganteaume does not possess either the intriguing character of Truguet or the valorous one of Villeneuve.

Before the Revolution he was a mate of a merchantman, but when most of the officers of the former royal navy had emigrated or perished, he was, in 1793, made a captain of the republican navy, and in 1796 an admiral. During the battle of Aboukir he was the chief of the staff, under Admiral Brueys, and saved himself by swimming, when l'Orient took fire and blew up. Bonaparte wrote to him on this occasion: "The picture you have sent me of the disaster of l'Orient, and of your own dreadful situation, is horrible; but be assured that, having such a miraculous escape, DESTINY intends you to avenge one day our navy and our friends." This note was written in August, 1798, shortly after Bonaparte had professed himself a Mussulman.

When, in the summer of 1799, our general-in-chief had determined to leave his army of Egypt to its destiny, Ganteaume equipped and commanded the squadron of frigates which brought him to Europe, and was, after his consulate, appointed a Counsellor of State and commander at Brest. In 1800 he escaped with a division of the Brest fleet to Toulon, and, in the summer of 1801, when he was ordered to carry succours to Egypt, your ship Skitsure fell in with him, and was captured. As he did not, however, succeed in landing in Egypt the troops on board his ships, a temporary disgrace was incurred, and he was deprived of the command, but made a maritime prefect. Last year favour was restored him, with the command of our naval forces at Brest. All officers who have served under Ganteaume agree that, let his fleet be ever so superior, he will never fight if he can avoid it, and that, in orderly times, his capacity would, at the utmost, make him regarded as a good master of a merchantman, and nothing else.

Of the present commander of our, flotilla at Boulogne, Lacrosse, I will also say some few words. A lieutenant before the Revolution, he became, in 1789, one of the most ardent and violent Jacobins, and in 1792 was employed by the

friend of the Blacks, and our Minister, Monge, as an emissary in the West
Indies, to preach there to the negroes the rights of man and insurrection
against the whites, their masters. In 1800, Bonaparte advanced him to a
captain-general at Guadeloupe, an island which his plots, eight years before,
had involved in all the horrors of anarchy, and where, when he now attempted
to restore order, his former instruments rose against him and forced him to
escape to one of your islands—I believe Dominico. Of this island, in return
for his hospitable reception, he took plans, according to which our General
Lagrange endeavoured to conquer it last spring. Lacrosse is a perfect
revolutionary fanatic, unprincipled, cruel, unfeeling, and intolerant. His
presumption is great, but his talents are trifling.

LETTER XXXIV.

PARIS, October, 1805.

MY LORD:—The defeat of the Austrians has excited great satisfaction among our courtiers and public functionaries; but the mass of the inhabitants here are too miserable to feel for anything else but their own sufferings. They know very well that every victory rivets their fetters, that no disasters can make them more heavy, and no triumph lighter. Totally indifferent about external occurrences, as well as about internal oppressions, they strive to forget both the past and the present, and to be indifferent as to the future; they would be glad could they cease to feel that they exist. The police officers were now, with their gendarmes, bayoneting them into illuminations for Bonaparte's successes, as they dragooned them last year into rejoicings for his coronation. I never observed before so much apathy; and in more than one place I heard the people say, "Oh! how much better we should be with fewer victories and more tranquillity, with less splendour and more security, with an honest peace instead of a brilliant war." But in a country groaning under a military government, the opinions of the people are counted for nothing.

At Madame Joseph Bonaparte's circle, however, the countenances were not so gloomy. There a real or affected joy seemed to enliven the usual dullness of these parties; some actors were repeating patriotic verses in honour of the victor; while others were singing airs or vaudevilles, to inspire our warriors with as much hatred towards your nation as gratitude towards our Emperor. It is certainly neither philosophical nor philanthropical not to exclude the vilest of all passions, HATRED, on such a happy occasion. Martin, in the dress of a conscript, sang six long couplets against the tyrants of the seas; of which I was only able to retain the following one:

Je deteste le peuple anglais, Je deteste son ministere; J'aime l'Empereur des Francais, J'aime la paix, je hais la guerre; Mais puisqu'il faut la soutenir Contre une Nation Sauvage, Mon plus doux, mon plus grand desir Est de montrer tout mon courage.

But what arrested my attention, more than anything else which occurred in this circle on that evening, was a printed paper mysteriously handed about, and of which, thanks to the civility of a Counsellor of State, I at last got a sight. It was a list of those persons, of different countries, whom the Emperor of the French has fixed upon, to replace all the ancient dynasties of Europe within twenty years to come. From the names of these individuals, some of whom are known to me, I could perceive that Bonaparte had more difficulty to select proper Emperors, Kings, and Electors, than he would have had, some years ago, to choose directors or consuls. Our inconsistency is, however, evident even here; I did not read a name that is not found in the annals of Jacobinism and republicanism. We have, at the same time, taken care not to forget ourselves in this new distribution of supremacy. France is to furnish the stock of the new dynasties for Austria, England, Spain, Denmark, and Sweden. What would you think, were you to awake one morning the subject of King Arthur O'Connor the First? You would, I dare say, be even more surprised than I am in being the subject of Napoleon Bonaparte the First. You know, I suppose, that O'Connor is a general of division, and a commander of the Legion of Honour,—the bosom friend of Talleyrand, and courting, at this moment, a young lady, a relation of our Empress, whose portion may one day be an Empire. But I am told that, notwithstanding Talleyrand's recommendations, and the approbation of Her Majesty, the lady prefers a colonel, her own countryman, to the Irish general. Should, however, our Emperor announce his determination, she would be obliged to marry as he commands, were he even to give her his groom, or his horse, for a spouse.

You can form no idea how wretched and despised all the Irish rebels are here. O'Connor alone is an exception; and this he owes to Talleyrand, to General Valence, and to Madame de Genlis; but even he is looked on with a sneer, and, if he ever was respected in England, must endure with poignancy the contempt to which he is frequently exposed in France. When I was in your country I often heard it said that the Irish were generally considered as a debased and perfidious people, extremely addicted to profligacy and drunkenness, and, when once drunk, more cruelly ferocious than even our Jacobins. I thought it then, and I still believe it, a national prejudice, because I am convinced that the vices or virtues of all civilized nations are relatively the same; but those Irish rebels we have seen here, and who must be, like our Jacobins, the very dregs of their country, have conducted themselves so as to inspire not only mistrust but abhorrence. It is also an undeniable truth that they were greatly disappointed by our former and present Government. They expected to enjoy liberty and equality, and a pension for their treachery; but our police commissaries caught them at their landing, our gendarmes escorted them as criminals to their place of destination, and there they received just enough to prevent them from starving. If they complained they were put in irons, and if they attempted to escape they were sent to the galleys as malefactors or shot as spies. Despair, therefore, no doubt induced many to perpetrate acts of which they were accused, and to rob, swindle, and murder, because they were punished as thieves and assassins. But, some of them, who have been treated in the most friendly, hospitable, and generous manner in this capital, have proved themselves ungrateful, as well as infamous. A lady of my acquaintance, of a once large fortune, had nothing left but some furniture, and her subsistence depended upon what she got by letting furnished lodgings. Mischance brought three young Irishmen to her house, who pretended to be in daily expectation of remittances from their country, and of a pension from Bonaparte. During six months she not only lodged and supported them, but embarrassed herself to procure them linen and a decent apparel. At last she was informed that each of, them had been allowed sixty livres—in the month, and that arrears had been paid them for nine months. Their debt to her was above three thousand livres—but the day after she asked for payment they decamped, and one of them persuaded her daughter, a girl of fourteen, to elope with him, and to assist him in robbing her mother of all her plate.—He has, indeed, been since arrested and sentenced to the galleys for eight years; but this punishment neither restored the daughter her virtue nor the mother her property. The other two denied their debts, and, as she had no other evidence but her own scraps of accounts, they could not be forced to pay; their obdurate effrontery and infamy, however, excited such an indignation in the judges, that they delivered them over as swindlers to the Tribunal Correctional; and the Minister of Police ordered them to be transported as rogues and vagabonds to the colonies. The daughter died shortly after, in consequence of a miscarriage, and the mother did not survive her more than a month, and ended her days in the Hotel Dieu, one of our common hospitals. Thus, these depraved young men ruined and murdered their benefactress and her child; and displayed, before they were thirty, such a consummate villainy as few wretches grown hoary in vice have perpetrated. This act of scandalous notoriety injured the Irish reputation very much in this country; for here, as in many other places, inconsiderate people are apt to judge a whole nation according to the behaviour of some few of its outcasts.

LETTER XXXV.

PARIS, October, 1805.

MY LORD:—The plan of the campaign of the Austrians is incomprehensible to all our military men—not on account of its profundity, but on account of its absurdity or incoherency. In the present circumstances, half-measures must always be destructive, and it is better to strike strongly and firmly than justly. To invade Bavaria without disarming the Bavarian army, and to enter Suabia and yet acknowledge the neutrality of Switzerland, are such political and military errors as require long successes to repair, but which such an enemy as Bonaparte always takes care not to leave unpunished.

The long inactivity of the army under the Archduke Charles has as much surprised us as the defeat of the army under General von Mack; but from what I know of the former, I am persuaded that he would long since have pushed forward had not his movements been unfortunately combined with those of the latter. The House of Lorraine never produced a more valiant warrior, nor Austria a more liberal or better instructed statesman, than this Prince. Heir to the talents of his ancestors, he has commanded, with glory, against France during the revolutionary war; and, although he sometimes experienced defeats, he has rendered invaluable services to the chief of his House by his courage, by his activity, by his constancy, and by that salutary firmness which, in calling the generals and superior officers to their duty, has often reanimated the confidence and the ardour of the soldier.

The Archduke Charles began, in 1793, his military career under the Prince of Coburg, the commander-in-chief of the Austrian armies in Brabant, where he commanded the advanced guard, and distinguished himself by a valour sometimes bordering on temerity, but which, by degrees, acquired him that esteem and popularity, among the troops often very advantageous to him afterwards. He was, in 1794, appointed governor and captain-general of the Low Countries, and a Field-marshal lieutenant of the army of the German Empire. In April, 1796, he took the command-in-chief of the armies of Austria and of the Empire, and, in the following June, engaged in several combats with General Moreau, in which he was repulsed, but in a manner that did equal honour to the victor and to the vanquished.

The Austrian army on the Lower Rhine, under General Wartensleben, having, about this time, been nearly dispersed by General Jourdan, the Archduke left some divisions of his forces under General Latour, to impede the progress of Moreau, and went with the remainder into Franconia, where he defeated

Jourdan near Amberg and Wurzburg, routed his army entirely, and forced him to repass the Rhine in the greatest confusion, and with immense loss. The retreat of Moreau was the consequence of the victories of this Prince. After the capture of Kehl, in January, 1797, he assumed the command of the army of Italy, where he in vain employed all his efforts to put a stop to the victorious progress of Bonaparte, with whom, at last, he signed the preliminaries of peace at Leoben. In the spring of 1799, he again defeated Jourdan in Suabia, as he had done two years before in Franconia; but in Switzerland he met with an abler adversary in General Massena; still, I am inclined to think that he displayed there more real talents than anywhere else; and that this part of his campaign of 1799 was the most interesting, in a military point of view.

The most implacable enemies of the politics of the House of Austria render justice to the plans, to the frankness, to the morality of Archduke Charles; and, what is remarkable, of all the chiefs who have commanded against revolutionary France, he alone has seized the true manner of combating enthusiasts or slaves; at least, his proclamations are the only ones composed with adroitness, and are what they ought to be, because in them an appeal is made to the public opinion at a time when opinion almost constitutes half the strength of armies.

The present opposer of this Prince in Italy is one of our best, as well as most fortunate, generals. A Sardinian subject, and a deserter from the Sardinian troops, he assisted, in 1792, our commander, General Anselm, in the conquest of the county of Nice, rather as a spy than as a soldier. His knowledge of the Maritime Alps obtained, in 1793, a place on our staff, where, from the services he rendered, the rank of a general of brigade was soon conferred on him. In 1796 he was promoted to serve as a general of division under Bonaparte in Italy, where he distinguished himself so much that when, in 1798, General Berthier was ordered to accompany the army of the East to Egypt, he succeeded him as commander-in-chief of our troops in the temporary Roman Republic. But his merciless pillage, and, perhaps, the idea of his being a foreigner, brought on a mutiny, and the Directory was obliged to recall him. It was his campaign in Switzerland of 1799, and his defence of Genoa in 1800, that principally ranked him high as a military chief. After the battle of Marengo he received the command of the army of Italy; but his extortions produced a revolt among the inhabitants, and he lived for some time in retreat and disgrace, after a violent quarrel with Bonaparte, during which many severe truths were said and heard on both sides.

After the Peace of Luneville, he seemed inclined to join Moreau, and other discontented generals; but observing, no doubt, their want of views and union, he retired to an estate he has bought near Paris, where Bonaparte visited him, after the rupture with your country, and made him, we may conclude, such offers as tempted him to leave his retreat. Last year he was nominated one of our Emperor's Field-marshals, and as such he relieved Jourdan of the command in the kingdom of Italy. He has purchased with a part of his spoil, for fifteen millions of livres—property in France and Italy; and is considered worth double that sum in jewels, money, and other valuables.

Massena is called, in France, the spoiled child of fortune; and as Bonaparte, like our former Cardinal Mazarin, has more confidence in fortune than in merit, he is, perhaps, more indebted to the former than to the latter for his present situation; his familiarity has made him disliked at our Imperial Court, where he never addresses Napoleon and Madame Bonaparte as an Emperor or an Empress without smiling.

General St. Cyr, our second in command of the army of Italy, is also an officer of great talents and distinctions. He was, in 1791, only a cornet, but in 1795, he headed, as a general, a division of the army of the Rhine. In his report to the Directory, during the famous retreat of 1796, Moreau speaks highly of this general, and admits that his. achievements, in part, saved the republican army. During 1799 he served in Italy, and in 1800 he commanded the centre of the army of the Rhine, and assisted in gaining the victory of Hohenlinden. After the Peace of Lundville, he was appointed a Counsellor of State of the military section, a place he still occupies, notwithstanding his present employment. Though under forty years of age, he is rather infirm, from the fatigues he has undergone and the wounds he has received. Although he has never combated as a general-in-chief, there is no doubt but that he would fill such a place with honour to himself and advantage to his country.

Of the general officers who command under Archduke Charles, Comte de Bellegarde is already known by his exploits during the last war. He had distinguished himself already in 1793, particularly when Valenciennes and Maubeuge were besieged by the united Austrian and English forces; and, in 1794, he commanded the column at the head of which the Emperor marched, when Landrecy was invested. In 1796, he was one of the members of the Council of the Archduke Charles, when this Prince commanded for the first time as a general-in-chief, on which occasion he was promoted to a Field-marshal lieutenant.

He displayed again great talents during the campaign of 1799, when he headed a small corps, placed between General Suwarow in Italy, and Archduke Charles in Switzerland; and in this delicate post he contributed equally to the success of both. After the Peace of Luneville he was appointed a commander-in-chief for the Emperor in the ci-devant Venetian States, where the troops composing the army under the Archduke Charles were, last summer, received and inspected by him, before the arrival of the Prince. He is considered by military men as greatly superior to most of the generals now employed by the Emperor of Germany.

LETTER XXXVI.

PARIS, October, 1805.

MY LORD:—"I would give my brother, the Emperor of Germany, one further piece of advice. Let him hasten to make peace. This is the crisis when, he must recollect, all States must have an end. The idea of the approaching extinction of the, dynasty of Lorraine must impress him with horror." When Bonaparte ordered this paragraph to be inserted in the Moniteur, he discovered an 'arriere pensee', long suspected by politicians, but never before avowed by himself, or by his Ministers. "That he has determined on the universal change of dynasties, because a usurper can never reign with safety or honour as long as any legitimate Prince may disturb his power, or reproach him for his rank." Elevated with prosperity, or infatuated with vanity and pride, he spoke a language which his placemen, courtiers, and even his brother Joseph at first thought premature, if not indiscreet. If all lawful Sovereigns do not read in these words their proscription, and the fate which the most powerful usurper that ever desolated mankind has destined for them, it may be ascribed to that blindness with which Providence, in its wrath, sometimes strikes those doomed to be grand examples of the vicissitudes of human life.

"Had Talleyrand," said Louis Bonaparte, in his wife's drawing-room, "been by my brother's side, he would not have unnecessarily alarmed or awakened those whom it should have been his policy to keep in a soft slumber, until his blows had laid them down to rise no more; but his soldier-like frankness frequently injures his political views." This I myself heard Louis say to Abbe Sieyes, though several foreign Ambassadors were in the saloon, near enough not to miss a word. If it was really meant as a reflection on Napoleon, it was imprudent; if designed as a defiance to other Princes, it was unbecoming and impertinent. I am inclined to believe it, considering the individual to whom it was addressed, a premeditated declaration that our Emperor expected a universal war, was prepared for it, and was certain of its fortunate issue.

When this Sieyes is often consulted, and publicly flattered, our politicians say, "Woe to the happiness of Sovereigns and to the tranquillity of subjects; the fiend of mankind is busy, and at work," and, in fact, ever since 1789, the infamous ex-Abbe has figured, either as a plotter or as an actor, in all our dreadful and sanguinary revolutionary epochas. The accomplice of La Fayette in 1789, of Brissot in 1791, of Marat in 1792, of Robespierre in 1793, of Tallien in 1794, of Barras in 1795, of Rewbel in 1797, and of Bonaparte in 1799, he has hitherto planned, served, betrayed, or deserted all factions. He is one of the few of our grand criminals, who, after enticing and sacrificing his associates, has been fortunate enough to survive them. Bonaparte has heaped upon him presents, places, and pensions; national property, senatories, knighthoods, and palaces; but he is, nevertheless, not supposed one of our Emperor's most dutiful subjects, because many of the late changes have differed from his metaphysical schemes of innovation, of regeneration, and of overthrow. He has too high an opinion of his own deserts not to consider it beneath his philosophical dignity to be a contented subject of a fellow-subject, elevated into supremacy by his labours and dangers. His modesty has, for these sixteen years past, ascribed to his talents all the glory and prosperity of France, and all her misery and misfortunes to the disregard of his counsels, and to the neglect of his advice. Bonaparte knows it; and that he is one of those crafty, sly, and dark conspirators, more dangerous than the bold assassin, who, by sophistry, art, and perseverance insinuate into the minds of the unwary and daring the ideas of their plots, in such an insidious manner that they take them and foster them as the production of their own genius; he is, therefore, watched by our Imperial spies, and never consulted but when any great blow is intended to be struck, or some enormous atrocities perpetrated. A month before the seizure of the Duc d'Enghien, and the murder of Pichegru, he was every day shut up for some hours with Napoleon Bonaparte at St. Cloud, or in the Tuileries; where he has hardly been seen since, except after our Emperor's return from his coronation as a King of Italy.

Sieyes never was a republican, and it was cowardice alone that made him vote for the death of his King and benefactor; although he is very fond of his own metaphysical notions, he always has preferred the preservation of his life to the profession or adherence to his systems. He will not think the Revolution complete, or the constitution of his country a good one, until some Napoleon, or some Louis, writes himself an Emperor or King of France, by the grace of Sieyes. He would expose the lives of thousands to obtain such a compliment to his hateful vanity and excessive pride; but he would not take a step that endangered his personal safety, though it might eventually lead him to the possession of a crown.

From the bounty of his King, Sieyes had, before the Revolution, an income of fifteen thousand livres—per annum; his places, pensions, and landed estates produce now yearly five hundred thousand livres—not including the interest of his money in the French and foreign funds.

Two years ago he was exiled, for some time, to an estate of his in Touraine, and Bonaparte even deliberated about transporting him to Cayenne, when Talleyrand observed "that such a condemnation would endanger that colony of France, as he would certainly organize there a focus of revolutions, which might also involve Surinam and the Brazils, the colonies of our allies, in one common ruin. In the present circumstances," added the Minister, "if Sieyes is to be transported, I wish we could land him in England, Scotland, or Ireland, or even in Russia."

I have just heard from a general officer the following anecdote, which he read to me from a letter of another general, dated Ulm, the 25th instant, and, if true, it explains in part Bonaparte's apparent indiscretion in the threat thrown out against all ancient dynasties.

Among his confidential generals (and hitherto the most irreproachable of all our military commanders), Marmont is particularly distinguished. Before Napoleon left this capital to head his armies in Germany, he is stated to have sent despatches to all those traitors dispersed in different countries whom he has selected to commence the new dynasties, under the protection of the Bonaparte Dynasty. They were, no doubt, advised of this being the crisis when they had to begin their machinations against thrones. A courier from Talleyrand at Strasburg to Bonaparte at Ulm was ordered to pass by the corps under the command of Marmont, to whom, in case the Emperor had advanced too far into Germany, he was to deliver his papers. This courier was surprised and interrupted by some Austrian light troops; and, as it was only some few hours after being informed of this capture that Bonaparte expressed himself frankly, as related above, it was supposed by his army that the Austrian Government had already in its power despatches which made our schemes of improvement at Paris no longer any secrets at Vienna. The writer of this letter added that General Marmont was highly distressed on account of this accident, which might retard the prospect of restoring to Europe its long lost peace and tranquillity.

This officer made his first campaign under Pichegru in 1794, and was, in 1796, appointed by Bonaparte one of his aides-de-camp. His education had been entirely military, and in the practice the war afforded him he soon evinced how well he remembered the lessons of theory. In the year 1796, at the battle of Saint-Georges, before Mantua, he charged at the head of the eighth battalion of grenadiers, and contributed much to its fortunate issue. In October of the same year, Bonaparte, as a mark of his satisfaction, sent him to present to the Directory the numerous colours which the army of Italy had conquered; from whom he received in return a pair of pistols, with a fraternal hug from Carnot. On his return to Italy he was, for the first time, employed by his chief in a political capacity. A republic, and nothing but a republic, being then the order of the day, some Italian patriots were convoked at Reggio to arrange a plan for a Cisalpine Republic, and for the incorporation with it of

Modena, Bologna, and other neutral States; Marmont was nominated a French republican plenipotentiary, and assisted as such in the organization of a Commonwealth, which since has been by turns a province of Austria or a tributary State of France.

Marmont, though combating for a bad cause, is an honest man; his hands are neither soiled with plunder, nor stained with blood. Bonaparte, among his other good qualities, wishes to see every one about him rich; and those who have been too delicate to accumulate wealth by pillage, he generally provides for, by putting into requisition some great heiress. After the Peace of Campo Formio, Bonaparte arrived at Paris, where he demanded in marriage for his aide-de-camp Marmont, Mademoiselle Perregeaux, the sole child of the first banker in France, a well-educated and accomplished young lady, who would be much more agreeable did not her continual smiles and laughing indicate a degree of self-satisfaction and complacency which may be felt, but ought never to be published.

The banker, Perregeaux, is one of those fortunate beings who, by drudgery and assiduity, has succeeded in some few years to make an ample fortune. A Swiss by birth, like Necker, he also, like him, after gratifying the passion of avidity, showed an ambition to shine in other places than in the counting-house and upon the exchange. Under La Fayette, in 1790, he was the chief of a battalion of the Parisian National Guards; under Robespierre, a commissioner for purchasing provisions; and under Bonaparte he is become a Senator and a commander of the Legion of Honour. I am told that he has made all his money by his connection with your country; but I know that the favourite of Napoleon can never be the friend of Great Britain. He is a widower; but Mademoiselle Mars, of the Emperor's theatre, consoles him for the loss of his wife.

General Marmont accompanied Bonaparte to Egypt, and distinguished himself at the capture of Malta, and when, in the following year, the siege of St. Jean d'Acre was undertaken, he was ordered to extend the fortifications of Alexandria; and if, in 1801, they retarded your progress, it was owing to his abilities, being an officer of engineers as well as of the artillery. He returned with Bonaparte to Europe, and was, after his usurpation, made a Counsellor of State. At the battle of Marengo he commanded the artillery, and signed afterwards, with the Austrian general, Count Hohenzollern, the Armistice of Treviso, which preceded shortly the Peace of Luneville. Nothing has abated Bonaparte's attachment to this officer, whom he appointed a commander-in-chief in Holland, when a change of Government was intended there, and whom he will entrust everywhere else, where sovereignty is to be abolished, or thrones and dynasties subverted.

LETTER XXXVII.

PARIS, October, 1805.

MY LORD:—Many wise people are of the opinion that the revolution of another great Empire is necessary to combat or oppose the great impulse occasioned by the Revolution of France, before Europe can recover its long-lost order and repose. Had the subjects of Austria been as disaffected as they are loyal, the world might have witnessed such a terrible event, and been enabled to judge whether the hypothesis was the production of an ingenious schemer or of a profound statesman. Our armies under Bonaparte have never before penetrated into the heart of a country where subversion was not prepared, and where subversion did not follow.

How relatively insignificant, in the eyes of Providence, must be the independence of States and the liberties of nations, when such a relatively insignificant personage as General von Mack can shake them? Have, then, the Austrian heroes—a Prince Eugene, a Laudon, a Lasci, a Beaulieu, a Haddick, a Bender, a Clairfayt, and numerous other valiant and great warriors—left no posterity behind them; or has the presumption of General von Mack imposed upon the judgment of the Counsellors of his Prince? This latter must have been the case; how otherwise could the welfare of their Sovereign have been entrusted to a military quack, whose want of energy and bad disposition had, in 1799, delivered up the capital of another Sovereign to his enemies. How many reputations are gained by an impudent assurance, and lost when the man of talents is called upon to act and the fool presents himself.

Baron von Mack served as an aide-de-camp under Field-marshal Laudon, during the last war between Austria and Turkey, and displayed some intrepidity, particularly before Lissa. The Austrian army was encamped eight leagues from that place, and the commander-in-chief hesitated to attack it, believing it to be defended by thirty thousand men. To decide him upon making this attack, Baron von Mack left him at nine o'clock at night, crossed the Danube, accompanied only by a single Uhlan, and penetrated into the suburb of Lissa, where he made prisoner a Turkish officer, whom, on the next morning at seven o'clock, he presented to his general, and from whom it was learnt that the garrison contained only six thousand, men. This personal temerity, and the applause of Field-marshal Laudon, procured him then a kind of reputation, which he has not since been able to support. Some theoretical knowledge of the art of war, and a great facility of conversing on military topics, made even the Emperor Joseph conceive a high opinion of this officer; but it has long been proved, and experience confirms it every day, that the difference is immense between the speculator and the operator, and that the generals of Cabinets are often indifferent captains when in the camp or in the field.

Preceded by a certain celebrity, Baron von Mack served, in 1793, under the Prince of Coburg, as an adjutant-general, and was called to assist at the Congress at Antwerp, where the operations of the campaign were regulated. Everywhere he displayed activity and bravery; was wounded twice in the month of May; but he left the army without having performed anything that evinced the talents which fame had bestowed on him. In February, 1794, the Emperor sent him to London to arrange, in concert with your Government, the plans of the campaign then on the eve of being opened; and when he returned to the Low Countries he was advanced to a quartermaster-general of the army of Flanders, and terminated also this unfortunate campaign without having done anything to justify the reputation he had before acquired or usurped. His Sovereign continued, nevertheless, to employ him in different armies; and in January, 1797, he was appointed a Field-marshal lieutenant and a quartermaster-general of the army of the Rhine. In February he conducted fifteen thousand of the troops of this army to reinforce the army of Italy; but when Bonaparte in April penetrated into Styria and Carinthia, he was ordered to Vienna as a second in command of the levy 'en masse'.

Real military characters had already formed their opinion of this officer, and saw a presumptuous charlatan where others had admired an able warrior. His own conduct soon convinced them that they neither had been rash nor mistaken. The King of Naples demanding, in 1798, from his son-in-law, the Emperor of Germany, a general to organize and head his troops, Baron von Mack was presented to him. After war had been declared against France he obtained some success in partial engagements, but was defeated in a general battle by an enemy inferior in number. In the Kingdom of Naples, as well as in the Empire of Germany, the fury of negotiation seized him when he should have fought, and when he should have remembered that no compacts can ever be entered into with political and military earthquakes, more than with physical ones. This imprudence, particularly as he was a foreigner, excited suspicion among his troops, whom, instead of leading to battle, he deserted, under the pretence that his life was in danger, and surrendered himself and his staff to our commander, Championnet.

A general who is too fond of his life ought never to enter a camp, much less to command armies; and a military chief who does not consider the happiness and honour of the State as his first passion and his first duty, and prefers existence to glory, deserves to be shot as a traitor, or drummed out of the army as a dastardly coward. Without mentioning the numerous military faults committed by General von Mack during this campaign, it is impossible to deny that, with respect to his own troops, he conducted himself in the most pusillanimous manner. It has often been repeated that martial valour does not always combine with it that courage and that necessary presence of mind which knows how to direct or repress multitudes, how to command obedience and obtain popularity; but when a man is entrusted with the safety of an Empire, and assumes such a brilliant situation, he must be weak-minded and despicable indeed, if he does not show himself worthy of it by endeavouring to succeed, or perish in the attempt. The French emigrant, General Dumas, evinced what might have been done, even with the dispirited Neapolitan troops, whom he neither deserted, nor with whom he offered to capitulate.

Baron von Mack is in a very infirm state of health, and is often under the necessity of being carried on a litter; and his bodily complaints have certainly not increased the vigour of his mind. His love of life seems to augment in proportion as its real value diminishes. As to the report here of his having betrayed his trust in exchanging honour for gold, I believe it totally unfounded. Our intriguers may have deluded his understanding, but our traitors would never have been able to seduce or shake his fidelity. His head is weak, but his heart is honest. Unfortunately, it is too true that, in turbulent times, irresolution and weakness in a commander or a Minister operate the same, and are as dangerous as, treason.